A Vacation in Hell

Max Reede was warned about going to Hell Island, particularly about El Diablo Mountain. He said he always found these kinds of places were just stories to scare gullible people. It would be a cheap two weeks in a place that wasn't overrun with tourists. Voodoo and Hoodoo were silly superstitions. He doesn't have a superstitious bone in his body.

Then how do you explain this?

Contents

About the author

CD Moulton has traveled extensively over much of the world both in the music business, where he was a rock guitarist, songwriter and arranger and in an import/export business. He has been everything from a bar owner to auto salvage (junkyard) manager, longshoreman to high steel worker, orchid grower to landscaper, tropical fish farmer to commercial fisherman. He started writing books in 1983 and has published more than 350 books as of January 1, 2023. His most popular books to date are about research with orchids, though much of his science fiction and fantasy work has proven popular. He wrote the CD Grimes, PI series, and the Det. Nick Storie series, Clint Faraday series, and many other works.

He now resides in Gualaca, Chiriqui, Panamá, where he writes books, plays music with friends, does research with orchids and medicinal plants. He has lately become involved in fighting for the rights of the indigenous people, who are among his closest friends, and in fighting the extreme corruption in the courts and police in Panamá.

He offers the free e-book, *Fading Paradise*, that explains what he has been through because of the corruption.

CD is the discoverer of the Chadam Protocol for curing cancer.

Facebook page Ambrosia peruviana for cancer.

A Vacation in Hell

Bon Voyage Party

Max Reede Took the small envelope from his PO box. A small bit of mail. Didn't look like an ad. From Kitti French? Who the hell was Kitti French?

Oh, yeah. That dark fiery girl at Gene's party. The Halloween party. Goodlooking, and sexy as they come, but an attitude that turned him off within ten minutes of meeting her. Thought she was Queen of the May, or something. Whatever. One of Gene's weird friends. October 31, 2012, Celebrating the end of the world that was predicted to come in December – or something as goofy.

Gene would have weird friends. He was weird. Called himself a psychic student. Claimed he knew a true vampire, and was friends with several witches and warlocks.

Gene was from New Orleans. He spent a lot of time in Haiti and Jamaica. Eugene Lasalle. Mother was from Haiti, father was from Jamaica. Mother was part black and part French, father was

French.

Gene had taken on a plan to convince Max that the voodoo crap was real. That would be a losing proposition, from the get-go! Max didn't have a superstitious bone in his body. All that stuff was was trickery, theatrics, suggestion, and hypnotics. Kitti's atitude started the minute Gene told her Max didn't believe there was any truth to the voodoo stuff.

That was ... he didn't pay a lot of attention, but she was supposed to be an apprentice of something or other. He'd said something like, "It's not my thing to try to scam anyone. I prefer honest work. Sleep better that way." She got all huffy about him saying she was a phony.

Hell! He hadn't! He'd said it wasn't anything he would be interested in. Nothing personal.

He tore open the envelope. Fancy penmanship! She should get a job where that would mean something in this age of e-mail and computer generated ads.

Mr. Reede -

I don't know if you will remember me. We met at a party. You said you didn't believe in certain rites as practiced in the Caribbean.

I own a place where I spend some time on Hell Island. I very much doubt you have heard of it.

Hell Island is a typical tropical Caribbean

island. Palm trees and all that. Beautiful beaches, clean water, great fishing or snorkeling, surfing at some times of the year, very relaxed lifestyle. I always say the name of the place is like Greenland. The actual place is opposite what the name implies. The original settlers wished to do something to insure it would not be overrun with gaudy tourist traps and so forth.

I have a cabin on the water at Sunray Beach. It is a delightful place.

Make no mistake. There is much of what you call voodoo practiced there, but it is, as you will learn should you accept this offer, not an evil thing. It is more medicine and philosophy.

There are several there who do have a lot of power.

I propose that you take your vacation there. You have no one here, so Christmas in the Caribbean should appeal to you. Sun and palm trees instead of rain and frost. You will pay only for your food and so forth. You will only promise to care for the place as though it were your own. You will meet and know some very interesting people. Perhaps you will begin to understand us.

There is a place in the interior of the island where there are hundreds of tales of a great lurking evil. I think only that area is anyplace you would wish to avoid. While Hell Island is exactly one eighty from its name, El Diablo Mountain and the Valley of Lost Souls are truly descriptive. Should you challenge the old tales, it is on your own head.

I am aware that you took a dislike to me. I also reacted in that manner toward you. I very possibly was wrong, as were you, also. I make no claims of anything else. I feel you will wish to challenge the mountain and valley. I feel you will come back a different person, should you do so and survive.

There is the challenge, Mr. Reede! How will you answer it?

Should you accept this invitation, the party at Eugene's place Friday night can be your Bon Voyage party.

Will you be there? My crystal ball tells me you will.

Kitti French-

"A vacation on a Caribbean island, where all I pay for is food and, I imagine, transportation? You're on!"

"Well, Max! It seems you accept the challenge from Kitti! Welcome to your bon voyage party!" Gene greeted. "Come on in.

"Yo, everyone! The guest of honor has arrived! I'm too cheap for champagne, so bring out the beer!"

Kitti French came to grin at him. It wasn't what he expected, that it would be a sneering grin. It seemed more impish. They talked about the place. She said she was going there, by boat, Monday. He would be taken to the island when she went to get some things from the cabin, there. He could move right in.

"Monday?"

"Yes. Mama Bernadette said you would accept the challenge, and would be starting your vacation tomorrow, so would be ready. She's never wrong. She said to remember to bring your Glock, but you won't use it. It will make you feel more secure. Bring two tetracycline capsules. You will want them because of the change in water.

"I don't know what that means, but, as I said, she's never wrong. The rechargable batteries in your lantern will fail. They haven't been used much, so deteriorated. Because of this mention you will check them and bring new ones. You *will* want them. She says your life will be saved because you will bring snakeproof boots. There are snakes in the valley and on the mountain. You will encounter a bushmaster.

"That is all from her. She can't predict past that. You will come to points in your life where you must make a choice, and they will be choices you will meet, there. Your fate is determined at each one. Something on the mountain will be a major decision. If you don't meet and pass that point, you will never leave the mountain.

"I warn you about that. I don't wish to be the agent who brought you to your death. Please heed the warnings of Mama Bernadette. Me, I can be wrong. She is never wrong.

"I think you will survive, and will be a better person, one who has a greater understanding. I also think you will know emotions of an intensity you have never dreamed of."

"Yo! Kitti! Phone!" Gene called. She went to speak for a few minutes, then came back to say, "Mama Bernadette says to tell you to consider that a presence only she and two others have met will very possibility be there to meet you. She says to tell you it might be unwise for you to come. You will face a danger very few people have ever faced, directly. It will be a danger to your sanity. It will also be a direct danger to you in ways even she can't guess.

"Perhaps this was a bad idea, but she first said you would come. She said about the boots and ... I am confused. Mama Bernadette has never changed her mind, about anything. She says your very soul is in a period of flux. She can't predict. She doesn't ... I don't ... this was a bad idea! I meant to put you in a position where you would face truths, and would be taught a lesson, but ... I begin to fear this!"

Here goes the suggestion part, and the theatrics. Not gonna work, Honey! "Oh, I think I can handle it. We've gone this far, so I'll just go on. We'll see what happens."

She bit her lip, and shrugged. "Just so you understand that Mama Bernadette and I both think you shouldn't go. I'm completely serious. I didn't think it would come to anything like this!"

"I guess. What time Monday, and where?"

She told him the name of the boat, Sea Minor 7, and that it was in slip fourteen, at the marina. They would sail at six thirty. He wouldn't need a passport visa. There wasn't any government on Hell Island to check any such thing. He said he'd be there.

The party turned out to be fairly nice. He went home with Janice Linder.

He did have a few thoughts. Mama Bernadette did come up with a few things about him. A lot was logical progression. A few people carried tetracycline for when the change in diet and water left them with diarrhea. Kitti could have learned about most of it from friends, such as his Glock – but it was going to be a bit weird if his rechargable batteries actually were in bad shape. No one knew he even had the thing! It was true he hadn't used it in more than a year.

Don't start thinking about that kind of thing! The power of suggestion would be strengthened if he fell for the theatrics bit!

He'd get everything ready. He fully intended to have a good time on his vacation.

His rechargable batteries wouldn't hold a charge. He bought new ones.

The boat trip to the island was beautiful, and really very pleasant. He expected Kitti would keep up the suggestions, but she didn't, beyond saying she thought he really shouldn't go into the interior, for any reason. He got to where he kind of liked her. She had a good sense of humor, which always appealed to him in a person. She was more than average intelligent. She was really a knockout in a bathing suit.

They made the wharf at the little town of Puddle. Kitti had no idea of where the name came from. It was three forty five on Tuesday afternoon. He went to the only store there to buy enough food for a few days. She said to buy kerosene for the refrigerator. There was no electricity on the island, except the small generator at the store in town. The town was seven buildings used for whatever, and a dozen or so houses. Nothing was open, but the owner of the store came when Kitti called her. She was introduced as Mrs. Freeling. She just grunted when Max was introduced. She was a heavy woman in her late forties or early fifties, with a bad disposition, it seemed.

Jon LeMond had the ATV used to deliver anything that needed delivering. He said, "Grmpth." when introduced. Liam Desmond had the place that sold kerosene. He didn't acknowledge the introduction. He said he sold kerosene Wednesday and Saturday, but would sell him some today, because he was with Kitti, and he knew she had to go places a lot of the time. Seven fifty a gallon, cash. No credit.

Mark Renault, the captain of the boat, spoke to Kitti for a minute, then went to the boat and brought a five gallon can of kerosene after they left Jon's. He wouldn't need that much, but seven fifty was far too much. It was six to six and a quarter almost anywhere on those islands. The food had seemed cheap to him, but Kitti said they charged him about half again what they charged the natives. She had warned him that they didn't want visitors there. They would treat him a lot better when they learned he wouldn't be staying long.

The cabin was really very comfortable. It was almost a kilometer from the nearest neighbor – who he doubted would speak to him if they were close. That was probably a good thing. He wouldn't annoy anyone, and they wouldn't annoy him.

They quickly went through the cabin. Kitti explained whatever needed explaining. She got a few things to take back to the boat with her. When she was ready to leave, she took him out back of the cabin to point through the trees to El Diablo. She said the valley was just before.

"Max, I've gotten to know you a bit. I think you're a good person. Please forego the mountain.

"Here's Mama Bernadette's number. Call her before you do anything. Please! Please follow her advice about things. She really does have the power. Have a good vacation, meditate, or whatever, catch up on your swimming and fishing and beachcombing – okay?"

"I'll see how I feel about things tomorrow. No promises today. I want to get the feel of the place. I'll talk to Mama Bernadette."

She bit her lip, and nodded. He wished her bon voyage, and she and Mark got on the ATV trailer and left. He went inside, put his things in the bedroom, fired up the refrigerator, and went swimming. When he came back, a woman and teenage boy were sitting on the porch. He greeted them, and said his name was Max.

"What you want here, Mon?" the woman asked. She didn't bother to introduce herself or the boy.

"I wanted to have a nice vacation and study some things, but that might not happen. Everyone here's so damned rude."

She looked thoughtful, and nodded. "You got the guts to say what you think. Won't nobody bother you, you don't bother them first and don't bring others. This here ain't no tourist mecca, and ain't never gonna be.

"What you study mean somebody else comes here?"

"No."

"Good! I'm Lucy and he's Sam. Ain't the sociable type, but you done figured that, less you stupid. Heard Jon and come to see what's what. I got a place in there (she pointed toward the right and inland). Ain't nobody else close. Bout a kilometer."

"In the valley?"

"You daft er what?" Sam demanded. "Ain't nobody in the valley! Nobody alive, nohow! Don't nobody even go close to there! You goonie er what?"

"He ain't from here. He don't know nothin' bout the valley," Lucy said. "You gonna study in the valley?"

"I might. Maybe on the mountain, too!"

"Not just daft! Crazy as uh wankle bird!"

Max grinned at Sam. "You're not the first to say that!"

Sam laughed. "Probly not uh bad guy! Don't go

in there. You never come back. Six people I knowed of went in. One come back and dropped dead three days later! Off his head, total! Only one alive who come back from thuh mountin uz Mama Bernadette, but she got the power. She go to thuh valley some 'n talks with the dead, but she say it ain't thuh dead. She say they ain't from here 'n ain't dead's all."

"What does that mean?"

"Damned'f I know!" Max laughed, and said he wasn't so bad, either.

Lucy said they had to get home before dark. They left. Sam grinned and winked.

Max went inside to fix some supper. He wondered what that was about. Sam was a naturally friendly person. Lucy was beyond what he could figure.

Was she afraid of him? Why? Was she just, as she said, antisocial?

He was definitely going to have to speak with Mama Bernadette.

He laid out everything he felt he would need, watched the magnificent sunset, then sacked out for the night. There were strange noises, and he was pretty sure someone came to look in the windows. He had the Glock on the nightstand, within easy reach. He wasn't going to let this bunch scare him.

Actually, he was amused by what he figured was a bit of theatrics Kitti had set up to get him into a suggestible mood. He didn't think there was actual malice, anymore. This was more a fun thing with her that would convince him she actually did have voodoo powers.

Maybe she knew the methods and tricks, but that didn't mean power. There was evidence that some people had a sort of psy power, maybe Mama Bernadette. Not Kitti.

He wondered what Mama Bernasette would be like. Would she be a craggy hag with an evil eye, and all that shit?

He'd find out. Tomorrow.

Max got up to make a pot of coffee and have a glass of orange juice and a couple pancakes with guava jelly. He sat on the little porch facing the Caribbean to watch a sunrise that was easily as spectacular as the sunset had been last night.

He was very well-rested. There had been some noise during the night, but he didn't let it bother him. It was all what he expected on a tropical isle that was four fifths jungle. The cabin was more than comfortable.

The view from the little porch was toward the northeast. The cabin was back about eighty feet from the high tide line, and maybe sixty feet high on a low promontory. There were a few palm trees between him and the beach, which was a fairly wide band of pinkish sand. A pebble and small rock path led to the beach. There was a tiny island directly out, maybe a little more than half a mile, then open water to the horizon. Toward the left were some larger islands, but at a distance of more than ten miles, was his guess.

The tide was about half, he thought. The beach was fairly flat. Judging from when he first saw it at a lower level, the tide was probably only about two feet, at most. It was only a few days before the full moon, so the tides were at their highest level.

He took out his cell phone and was about to call Mama Bernadette, then thought about it.

Not smart! It was five minutes to six! He was always up early, but most people probably weren't! He'd wait until eight.

He went inside to heat the coffee and pour another cup, then went out the back to the little porch there. He could see El Diablo, looking like a typical tropical mountain, with a few light clouds below the peak. The form showed him it was probably a dead volcano.

There was a strange hooting sound from above, He searched through the trees to see two monkeys sitting there, watching him. He waved, and called, "Good morning!" They chattered at him, and soon went away. He grinned. It seemed he did have close neighbors – of sorts!

He went to sit again, and glanced toward El Diablo.

What the hell! The sky was a lime green! The mountain was a dark shape. It was downright surreal!

He shook his head, and looked at his coffee. Had someone come during the night and put some kind of hallucinogen in it?

No. It was vacuum sealed. The seal hadn't been broken when he opened it to make the coffee.

He didn't see how they worked that, but supposed they could be using something he absorbed, or in the air, or something.

He looked back at the mountain. It was normal and serene.

He went back inside to wash the cup and put everything back in place. He went to the little bathroom to shave and so forth, then put on a bathing suit. He would beachcomb for awhile, then call Mama Bernadette when he got back.

He went out on the porch, then stopped.

There were no locks on the door! He hadn't noticed when they came, but they just opened the door and came in!

He shook his head, and turned toward the path.

"There are no locks here. We have no thieves or such. I'm Bernadette LeGrange," a rather pretty woman, about 35, medium complexion, light brown hair, slightly plump, said. "You could have called at six. I awaken by five.

"The green view was because you were noted by ... people. It probably will not happen again. If you ... yes. You have a good memory, if not photographic. I remember when it happened for me. It is actually quite beautiful.

"You wished to consult with me. Kitti was more impressed than she would let you know. She is greatly afraid that you are in grave danger here – which you are. I am seldom confused by what you would call my talent. With you, I am very much confused. There are a minimum of three equal paths you may take, each with branches. You are the second person I have ever met who has no fixed future.

"I'm afraid I can give little advice until you select a path.

"I have seen until the moment you enter the valley. The first branch of the path is there. I can see very little of what would happen on either path."

"You obviously know who I am. You're nothing like I expected."

"Yes. People would think I'm an old crone who cackles a lot, or a flambouyant voodoo queen from the movies. I'm actually a rather normal sport of person with a talent."

"You seem educated. Your English is better than mine."

"Loyola, ninety nine. Master's in social science, if there really is such a thing."

"I am surprised. That has a lot more effect on my ideas than the theatricals and tricks. As Kitti probably told you, I don't believe in any of that stuff."

"Kitti didn't say, but I knew that when she asked if she could send you here to learn a lesson about the realities of the arts. I have to say most of it is trickery or chemicals, with some hypnotism thrown in. It does often depend on suggestion. A few people have a psy talent. We're born with it. They can study it all they like, but it can't be taught or learned. It's there, or it's not.

"You want to know about the mountain and valley. I can only say that the talent is of little use there, except communication. I have almost no knowledge of what is there, but it is not evil. It just ... is."

"My personal theory. Evil is in the use of a thing. Things are not evil or good. They just, as you said, are. A knife is not evil, only its use."

"A true bit of philosophy. If a knife is used to cut vegetables, it is not because it is good. If it is used to kill, it is not because it is evil. There is a correalisation with the valley. Because very few ever return who go there, it is not the fault of the valley. It is because of something that is there. My talent didn't save me after finding what it is, it kept me from being where I would encounter it. It was like something in my mind said I was not to take this or that trail. I avoided those places, and found nothing much bad in the valley. I felt there was great danger, but it was not evil, so I have no idea what it might have been.

"Have you heard of the theories of planal distortion? The kind of thing that well may be what the Devil's Triangle is about?"

"Yes. There is something such here? Is that what you're saying?"

"Yes and no. It would explain much. I think it may have something to do with the valley. I believe taking a certain path will lead to a certain fate. I feel that is why I cannot fathom your future. You haven't yet been fated to any definite path.

"If you are determined to go, as I see you are, trust your, what you call 'gut reactions,' in a given situation. Carry your lantern, though it is early morning. Wear your boots. Those things will happen."

"In the valley?"

"And just before."

"What about the mountain? What is there?"

"El Diablo is a dormant volcano. There are things there that ... there are things there. You will meet them, if you survive to reach the mountain. Do not react with fear, and there will be no need of it.

"If you do, I can tell you from personal exper-ience, do not go between the two arrowhead-shaped white rocks. Go to either side, and you will be in a place where you would not be if you go between them. You will just be on the mountain.

"I had a premonition, the first time I went there. I held the end of a string, so found my way back. Had I not done that, I would very likely have never returned here.

"I have no real knowledge of what I encountered there. I have what seem to be memories of meeting El Diablo, in person. That is the gate to hell. Other, I know exactly. It is for your exploration, not my saying.

"I have a personal theory that one passes into another reality when she goes between those rocks. That I met and spoke with El Diablo is most doubtful, but I did meet and speak with a strange being not of this world. I will not suggest what you may find if you go there. I am not certain I believe what I found will not impres you as truth.

"I studied Latin and Classical Greek at Loyola. I have to admit those languages proved very useful. I know you studied some Greek ... that your great grandmother was from Greece, that you learned to read the language to be able to read and understand the classical mythology. If you can put the proper sounds to the words, perhaps you will be able to communicate.

"There isn't much more I can tell you. I know my advice to forego a trip into the valley, thence to the mountain, should you survive, would be rejected.

"I will go back to Puddle, you will go to the valley.

"Take food for two days, minimum. There is plenty to be found in the valley, but – this part I don't know – it isn't all safe to eat. I know when a thing is not good. You have no such talent."

She changed the subject. They talked about the states and people she knew, then she headed back toward Puddle.

He got the things he would need to start on his little excursion.

He wasn't quite so flippant, after talking with Bernadette.

The first kilometer was fairly easy going, but the path ran out just before he reached the pass into the valley. It was obvious that no one had gone through there in quite a long time. The brush was impenetrable. He had to use a machette to cut a way in.

It took almost two hours to go through the pass, only about a kilometer. When he broke out the other side, the going was much easier. He stopped to look down on the lush valley with a small silver river winding along the bottom. El Diablo was magnificent, from that spot. It was a breathtaking vista.

He started to move forward when something hit his boot, only half an inch from the top. He saw a brownish snake with black X'es on the back. A bushmaster! Had he been wearing regular shoes, it would have bitten him! He was miles and hours away from any possible treatment. He would never have left the Valley of Lost Souls!

He decided not to chase it. It was a thing of the place. It was unlikely anyone else would come through to be threatened by it. He would certainly proceed with a lot more caution!

Fifteen minutes later, he came to a branch in the slight animal path he was taking. He saw they both went on downward, but one branch went more to the left, not so directly toward the mountain.

He almost started along the more direct path, but felt uneasy. He went back and down the other. He felt nothing unusual, there.

There was a mournful cry to his right. It sounded like ... nothing he had ever heard. A banshee? It sent a chill though him, and he felt the hair stand up on the back of his neck.

Did that other path lead to whatever made that cry?

He didn't really want to know. He did wonder if Mama Bernadette could read more of his future now.

What? He was getting brainwashed ... but she was right about the lantern batteries and the boots. He was glad he brought food and the lantern ... and his Glock. He had quite a lot of lightweight equipment in his special backpack.

He went on for an hour and a half, and came to the river. The water was clear and clean. There were tropical fishes of various types. He saw a school of yellowish-brown fish with bright scarlet throats.

Pirahnas? Here? Weren't they more an Amazon fish?

The water there was fairly deep. He wasn't about to go into it!

He could go either way along the river. It seemed more likely he would find a place to cross upstream, so he turned that way.

Another branch in the path. Would he have felt anything if he'd gone left instead of right?

He turned around, and started moving. He immediately felt something like ... he was being watched?

He looked down into the river. The pirahnas were there, moving along with him.

He turned back. The fish stopped. He started the other way. They didn't follow.

If he went down the river, would he come to whatever made that cry? Would he be forced to face it or the pirahnas?

Do *not* let your imagination get started here! He went on for twenty minutes or so and came to a rocky set of rapids. He could, with some difficulty, cross there.

He thought. He sat on a rock to eat one of his sandwiches and drink a can of peach nectar. He took the can and wrapper to drop into a plastic bag, which he hung on a strap to his backpack. He did not toss garbage on the ground. Ever.

He decided to go a bit more upriver to see if there was a better place to cross. He didn't think the pirahnas would come up the rapids, so the more between him and the unobstructed river, the better.

That was a good idea! He came to a swinging bridge across between two rises by the riverside!

A bridge? Where no one ever came? It didn't make sense – unless people did come. They were trying to stop him from coming, so the tales about the valley were just that. Tales.

Mama Bernadette. He took out his cellular, and saw there was a signal, if not too strong.

He called her. When she answered, he told her about what had happened, to that point. He asked about the bridge.

"Bridge? There is no bridge that I know about."

He described it.

"I can't see anything about you. I know you have taken two paths, both the safe ones. I don't know if the bridge is another choice you have to make. I didn't know of its existence.

"Max, I like you. I sense there is some kind of approval of you by someone or something indistinct. It has to do with you ... not ... dirtying something?"

"Not ... maybe because I ate a sandwich and

drank a canned drink, and didn't leave the garbage?"

"Perhaps. I can't advise you about the bridge."

"Would you cross it?"

There was a silence, then, "No."

"Then I won't. I'll call later, if there's a signal."

He went back up the river a short way until he found a place he could cross without too much trouble. He went slowly and very carefully across, then found a path toward the bridge, and another toward the mountain.

He didn't hesitate. He went toward the mountain.

It was fairly easy going. He was almost halfway between the river and mountain when it started getting dark. He was surprised, but his watch said it was nearly seven. He'd completely lost track of time!

He had the light plastic tent with an air matress bedroll sewn in under it. He set up the tent and inflated the bedroll with the little attached pump, then made a rocky pit for a fire. He soon had the fire going, so put on some water for coffee and brought out some paper and pencils to write about what he had seen. He had taken a lot of pictures, at first, not so many, later. The camera had a four gig card. He could take thousands, if he wanted. He had plenty of recharged batteries for the camera.

He opened a can of tuna and fried it, then cracked an egg over that. He put it between two slices of bread, and had a good sandwich.

He hadn't realized how tired he was. He went inside the tent and to sleep. It was a lot earlier than he was used to, but he would be up early. He wanted to be at the mountain before midday, if possible.

About three in the morning he was awakened by noises outside. He sat up, and turned on his lantern. He opened the flap, to find himself face-to-face with a large monkey or ape! He turned the lantern into the face, and it raced into the trees.

Pirahnas, now apes? Here? There were no apes on any Caribbean islands!

Was it an ape? It was a lot *like* an ape, but the features were ... different. It didn't seem to run hunched over like an ape.

He was very damned glad he had his Clock! He sure as Hell wasn't going to get more sleep tonight!

He was also glad Mama Bernadette said he wouldn't have to use the pistol. What if there were a colony of apes there, that he shot one – and the rest tore him to bloody little pieces?

Was the cry he'd heard from one of those apes? Were they why no one ever lived who came there? Were those stories true? Was he a total idiot to be here, against all advice?

He was down in the valley a distance. The sunrise was about twenty minutes later than on the beach. He saw it was six fifteen, and called Bernadette. There wasn't a signal there.

When it was light enough, he went outside, Glock in hand and ready, but there was nothing there, and no sign there had been anything.

Was it a nightmare? Was the suggestion getting through? How had any such idea been planted? *Had* it been planted?

No. There had been no suggestion of anything like that.

He brewed some coffee and had two eggs on toast, packed his backpack, and headed on toward the mountain. His mind was telling him to turn around and get the Hell out of there!

That wouldn't be him. He had come this far. He would finish the trip.

He came to the mountain, two hours later. It was on a slow rise, then suddenly was more steep. There was a path to the right, and one to the left.

What was with all these animal paths? There wasn't much to indicate there were any animals using them. They were just ... there. Were they made by the apes?

He checked his phone. There was a fair signal.

He called Bernadette. He got her, but there was a lot of static. He explained about his night, and the apes.

"They are not apes. There are no apes here."

"What are they?"

"That's the sixty four thousand dollar question. I never directly encountered any of them, but saw some evidence, and, one time, caught a glimpse of something. It seemed a very hairy and very large person. Only a glimpse, then it was gone. I sensed curiosity, not a threat. There may only be the one. There may be several. I don't know. I get no feeling about them. It."

"Well, I'm at the mountain. Should I go right or left?"

There was a silence. "I don't know."

They chatted for a minute, then the signal faded. Max put the phone back in the pocket sewn into the backpack and looked up and down the path. He shrugged, and went to the right. He came to a cave that the path led into. He shone his lantern into it, but didn't see anything but a lot of loose rock. There were rats in the cave. Maybe they made the path. He turned around, and went the opposite direction. More than an hour later, he came to two arrowhead-shaped white rocks.

<u>*El Diablo Mountain*</u>

Max took a lot of pictures. He took this spot from several angles. He remembered what Mama Bernadette said, so went to the left of the rocks to take pictures that looked exactly like the ones from just before. He went around to the other side to take more. No difference.

He went back to stand in front of the rocks. He remembered what Mama Bernadette said, so took out a long roll of nylon twine. It was on a reel spindle that he attached to a strong limb. He tied the end to his belt, took a deep breath, and stepped into the space between the rocks.

There was a blurry few seconds, then the light seemed to be far more toward the green. It was a little lighter than the lime green he saw in the flash, and was quite beautiful. The plants seemed of different types than were in the area.

He turned to look back the way he had come. The nylon line seemed to just begin a foot or so above the path, which went on out across a flatter area. No valley, no river.

He stepped back to where he found himself between the rocks, staring out across the valley.

This was weird! That planal distortion theory had to be right!

He turned around, and went back into the ... portal? There was three quarters of a mile on the reel. He was going to do a bit of exploring!

First things first. He needed to know where this spot was from this side. There were no arrowhead rocks here.

He noticed the path had a break where the line appeared. it was like a line of turquoise across the path. There seemed to be a slight fog on the path, right there.

He went around the path to the side. He could go on that way. He came back along the path, and was past the line. Apparently, you went through the portal in only one direction. He remembered that he had gone all the way around the rocks, finding no difference in the local landscape.

He went back to the path. He took two white pieces of cloth to tie to twigs on either side of the turquoise line. He stepped back behind the line to note they could be seen from either side of it. He then moved a couple hundred feet along the path, to see they were visible from a distance.

What now? Say he'd been to El Diablo Mountain, found an answer that led to dozens of new puzzles, and go home?

Yeah! Like he'd ever had that much sense! He

was here, and he was going to look for some answers.

He decided the best way to approach this was to move along that path. It was a lot more than the animal paths he had followed on the ... other side? This was mostly laid out with smaller pebbles poured in a line onto the sandy soil.

The plants were strange. Some were beautiful, some were odd, to the point of being scary. Flowers sometimes looked like bugs. He would use up the whole card if he took pictures at the rate he was going! He noticed there were a lot of thorny plants. He saw some bugs that were like nothing he'd ever imagined. The soil was a rich black, in this area, and his concentration was on random sweep, jumping from subject to subject.

There were a couple of little faint trails leading off to the sides. They didn't appear much used. They were probably animal paths, such as he followed on the other side. They looked like that.

He came to a rock wall. It was about eight feet high, with a wooden door across the path. A strange symbol was painted on the center panel.

Does that mean do not enter ... or do not exit? Is it advertising toothpaste, or something? Is it a for sale sign?

He took some pictures.

Decision time! Open that door, or turn back?

The smartest thing would be to see what he could before taking stupid chances

Maybe just open it and look?

What if there was an alarm attached ... or something?

He turned around. Why tempt fate?

He moved back a few feet when a figure stepped from one of the faint sidepaths. Its back was toward him, but he froze where he stood. He reached to take the Glock into his hand, then quickly pushed it back into its pocket on the backpack. Meeting a strange being with a weapon in your hand was a Hell of a long way from intelligent.

The being was moving away, but suddenly stopped, and spun to face him. It was a dark brown hairy being, very muscular, human-shaped. The fingernails and toenails were conical, just short of being claws. The face was as hairy as the body. The eyes were almost glowing, and were red. The mouth had two longer upper teeth among many sharp ones, almost fangs. This was a male – if not having teats meant anything here. All it was wearing was a sort of brief loincloth.

Okay. A male in Hell was a demon. This one looked the part!

The being made a short sort of growl, and moved toward Max. Max wished he'd kept the

Glock in his hand. He was as much as paralyzed from movement.

Why didn't he feel threatened? If there was ever a time in his life he should have felt sheer terror, this was it! Yet, he didn't feel he was in any particular danger.

The demon stopped about two yards from him. It seemed curious. It spoke in a language that really did, as Bernadette suggested, sound like Greek. He spoke a very little from when he spent two weeks in Athens, six years ago. He knew the classical Greek to read, and had noticed the vowel shifts and such in the language.

Nothing to lose. Try to remember the correct words and the correct structure of the sentence.

"Greetings! I am called Max. What are you called?"

The demon cocked his head to the side, and what could have been a grin crossed his face. "Octon. You ? a very strange ? You have crossed into ? by ? ? ?"

"I have too few words. I came across the portal."

The demon laughed. Why? What had he said?

"? you to encounter ? when ??. I do not ? while ??. I will then introduce ? and ? to ?? you. Come."

Max decided he liked this demon. He was more trying to help than threatening. Hell! *(Stop thinking with that word, here. It's where you are!*) He wasn't in the least threatening!

Max moved to beside the big demon, who spoke very little. He did say that the person(s) he would introduce could communicate much better.

Problem! His line was running out! He asked about that.

"You do not ? it. You can return here ? ?. We will ? to ??." He took the line to tie to a bright purple shrub. There were very few of those in the area, so he could locate it easily when (if) he came back.

They went on for more than a kilometer. The path was, it seemed, the only one that was paved with pebbles in the area.

They went into a small pleasant valley, and to a stone cabin. Octon waved him inside.

Octon was a demon who looked only a little like Max felt a demon would look. This one was a truly terrifying sight! He was a bit taller and more massively muscled than Octon, was deep black that set off the red eyes. He had longer fangs. He wasn't wearing the loincloth. There was certainly no doubt this was a male!

"This is Max, a ? ? came across the ?" Octon introduced. "Max, this is ? Arctus Julio.

"I will ?? to your ?" He waved, and left.

"Ah! Welcome to Hades, Max! Call me Juli," Juli said, in excellent English.

Max couldn't stop a short giggle. Juli asked why.

What the ... heck Be honest! "Juli somehow doesn't fit you."

Juli laughed. "Ah, yes! It is a woman's name, in your place! I am definitely not a woman!

"Have a seat. We can talk, then we can decide what to do with you. I think you'd be a bit tough, so dinner would probably not be a good idea."

Juli looked serious when he said that. Max didn't know how to react, so nodded, and said, "I agree. Not a good idea." He tried to look as serious as Juli.

Juli laughed. "You have a very good sense of humor in a situation that actually is very dangerous to you. You didn't threaten Octon, or anyone, or you would be dinner, but for the bugs and bacteria, not us. Probably. I can't speak for others.

"I don't understand why you, Kitti, and Bernadette didn't react to us in the way our races have historically acted. You are much like Bernadette, in thought. She was curious, and likes to make jokes. Kitti found us ... attractive, but frightening. You seem to be between those two.

"Bernadette taught me the English. We spend about fifty times the time people think together. We have developed a deep affection. We have a place we meet in the valley in a part where it is safe for both of us.

"You seem to desire honesty. I will say, directly and truly, that there have been forty two of your people who came here, and only Bernadette and Kitti have returned. There are several who came into the valley who did not return. The two or three who did return died within days. That is not from us. We have lost two of our people in that valley. We almost never go there. Bernadette and Kitti have a special path they use through the valley. I think they told you of it."

"No. Bernadette said I would come to forks in the path. It was to me to discover the correct one. I have a slight bit of her talent, I guess. I would get a definite feeling about which path to take. There were three that I somehow knew would be the bad choice. I could see why on one, particularly. Crossing the river. There were pirahnas in it. If I'd taken the other way, it would put me between the pirahnas and something pretty terrible. There's a bridge across the river. Bernadette said she would not take it – I was speaking with her on my phone – so I didn't."

"A bridge? Why would there be a bridge where no one ever goes? Bernadette and Kitti both sense there is something terrible there, but they feel it may not leave certain areas. The trick, as Kitti says, is to know which places to avoid.

"You do not wish to know why none of the others survived to return to your place?"

"I can assume they either threatened you with a

weapon or attacked you in another way, or died of heart failure. You are, after all, demons from Hell, in our legends!

"I considered showing a weapon when I first saw Octon. I felt that would be immensely stupid. It was a feeling like at the forks in the path. I was as much as paralyzed, but Octon merely seemed curious about me, and has a fun sense of humor. I immediately liked him.

"When I first saw you, my bones turned to jelly! Octon is a lot *like* the legends. You *are* the legend!"

Juli laughed. "Bernadette taught me a little joke. She said that I naturally would look like a demon from Hell. After all, I *are* one!"

Max laughed. He found he really did like these demons! They had great senses of humor.

"You have seen what happens when your people come here. Luckily, that is seldom. Long ago, one of our people, Dionysus, was killed, when two came through. He went to see what they were. He would have welcomed them here. We are a friendly and curious people. Since that time, we will defend ourselves, if attacked. We make no excuses.

"Bernadette has explained that the time and descriptions of the Dionysus encounter tells her a couple of pirates stumbled upon the portal. They were probably terrified, were very religious, they saw demons coming for their souls. They were wearing armor, and had weapons.

"Whatever, we make no apologies for defending ourselves. We are friendly people, who are capable of extreme violence."

"I think the problem started centuries ago. You speak what sounds very much like classical Greek. You are in the legends from that time, and before. There is some evidence that a few of us had a great deal more psy power back then than now. They discovered how to open a portal, and used your people to gain and hold power over others."

"It would agree much with our legends. The portals were opened. Something made three of them remain. Two are very large, and are fluctuating kinds of things. They are to other realities, not this one. Bernadette says one is called the Devil's Triangle, and is close to the place she was born. There are tales of mighty ships and areoplanes disappearing into those. She thinks there is a different time in those, that it is different from here.

"You have a lot of science. We have little. You are not a generally happy people, we are. Perhaps there is a connection, perhaps not. Bernadette says there is a different psychology. Kitti says you are a decadent society, based on greed. I know little of such things. Both she and Kitti say the real problem in your reality is that the race breeds like insects and rodents, with no consideration of the obvious facts that all of your race's problems are due to overpopulation.

"Perhaps that is because you have no cyclic fertile periods, as in our race. We have much the same reaction to sexual situations, but we avoid such relations when they will lead to such problems. You do not."

"We have fertile periods. We merely choose to not control anything. Most women, particularly among those who, logically, should not breed, want a lot of children. We know what the problem is. We refuse to do anything about it. We have contraceptives and painless sterilization methods, but generally ignore them.

"What a strange conversation!"

"Yes! Isn't it?"

Max couldn't help it! He liked these people, the two he'd met!

"Well, we will have some food, and will talk. You may wish to stay here the night, or go.

"I almost forgot! It would not be intentional. You cannot eat the food here. It will poison you."

"I have enough for two more meals. Dinner tonight, and breakfast tomorrow. That is no problem. I can spend the rest of today and awhile in the morning getting to know you. I think I very much like you demons from Hell!"

They stayed together. Juli introduced four others, two females. While they did not appeal to him, he could see how those into bondage and female dominance would find them as much as completely irresistible!

Max liked every one he met. They were open and curious. They found him odd and fun. They made jokes about him being the demon, not them! It was all goodnatured, not in any way hurtful.

He rested very well. He got some great pictures of the sunset and sunrise. Juli said the pictures wouldn't develop. He showed them the digital camera, and the pictures on the card. They noted the beauty of the sunrise and sunset, but the rest from there were ordinary. They were fascinated by the ones from his reality. The colors and forms were so different, mostly in subtle ways. The sunrise and sunset were such unusual colors!

About mid-morning, he headed back to the portal. Juli and Octon walked with him. They stepped out between the arrowhead rocks. This was the first time Octon had been outside his reality. He was fascinated, but nervous.

It seemed natural for him to hug these terrible monsters goodbye.

Max didn't waste much time on his way back. He came to the cabin, to find Bernadette and Kitti sitting on the porch, waiting for him. Kitti said Bernadette saw that he was welcomed by the people on the mountain.

"They aren't on a mountain, in their reality," he pointed out. "Just among some hills. The mountains were in the distance, there."

Bernadette wanted to know all about it, so he explained everything. She said it was all as she knew it to be, but there was no bridge that she remembered. There simply would be no point in having a bridge anywhere in a valley where no more than ten people went in ten years.

She had followed a different path to the mountain. She came on the river quite a distance upstream. It was where two creeks ran together to form the river. There were easy places to cross both creeks. There was no bad path up there.

"Whatever is wrong in that valley is more to this part," he suggested. "There's something there. Whatever it is is restricted as to where it can go. We took paths outside of its territory."

"That's a lot like what I felt," Bernadette replied. "Perhaps that bridge is at the limit of its area."

"I think I want to go back and cross that bridge. I'm damned well going to have the Glock in my hand, and it's going to have the safety off!"

"I don't sense any reason not to cross the bridge. It's there for another reason," Bernadette suggested. "I don't think you will need the gun, but you will ... there is something ... insane? There is something or someone insane there?

"Take the greatest care. I sense there is ... are ... two things there. The one makes you safe, but only because the other is there. It isn't clear. I can only express it as the insanity is no danger to you because the ... alienity? Is there."

"Then the insanity would be from this reality, the other not?" Kitti asked.

"That expresses it well."

Max thought, then nodded. "Tomorrow, for the bridge. Today, to lay around and download all my pictures. I wonder if the camera can capture the shades and tones there. I hope so."

"I sense that the pictures are proof only to you, that others will claim you have merely altered the colors."

"It's a good thing I'm the only one who cares about proof, and it'll be fine if it's only to me.

You two will know it's real."

"Different realities are what it's about," Kitti said, with a grin. He returned the grin.

Mama Bernadette said she would go back to Puddle. Kitti would stay. They could get to know each other. They would be friends, if not a lot more – but not to a level they couldn't both be comfortable. They would never love each other in any deeper emotional sense.

"More or less like you and Juli?"

"No. Juli and I take it to a far deeper place."

"But the Hadeans are great lovers!" Kitti said.

They joked a few more minutes, then Bernadette left, walking along the beach. Kitti went inside to cook a delicious meal. Max went swimming for awhile, had the meal, then cranked up his laptop to download the pictures. He used it for as little time as possible. He wanted to save the battery. He chatted and joked with Kitti. They strolled along the beach around the end of the island and back. That took three hours. They had a light meal, showered and such, then hit the sack – as Max hoped, by that time, together.

It was a great night!

In the morning, Max packed his backpack, made a few sandwiches, took some boxes of juices, and headed for the valley and the bridge. It was fairly fast going. He had followed that path both ways, so knew it. In a little less than two hours, he was standing by the bridge.

He suddenly felt danger behind him. He didn't hesitate to run across the bridge.

When he looked back, he didn't see anything ... or did he? He didn't remember passing that twisted driftwood tangle by the path! There wasn't any driftwood on the side of the mountain!

The "driftwood" moved to the end of the bridge. It didn't try to cross, though Max doubted it could. It was too big.

He took a series of pictures of the thing, part on zoom. The thing seemed to be looking for a way across the river. It raised itselt to about ten feet high, and made the horrible cry he had heard, it seemed, eons ago.

He turned to hurry along the path. He couldn't go back the way he came. He had to know where he could run if that thing crossed the river! Would it wait there?

Go on to the left. It wasn't back that way.

He was moving along a sort of cliff face when he came to a cave There was a small fire in a rocky bowl, with an old iron skillet on it. There was some kind of animal leg being fried in the skillet.

"It can't cross the river, young'un," a voice

close to his back said. He spun, to see a skinny old man with grey hair to below his shoulder-blades, holding a machette that was worn down to almost a thin sword.

"That's good to know! What in *Hell* is that thing?"

"Ha! That's a good one! What in *Hell* ... where we're at.

"I'm Carey. It's the devil, I think. Tryin' to get my soul fer more than fifty years now. Can't. Can't leave where God lets him roam. River here to thuh river over south to the mountain 'til the cliff up 'bout mebbe a thousand feet high. Can't go quite to thuh pits down there. Don't go under mebbe three hunderd feet high. People down there know to never go over that high. Don't never come, nohow. Only the ones the devil sends after me, but I know it's them. When they can't get me, he takes 'em. One done got away, and run back inta thuh town. Mind stayed up here. Body went back. Probly didn't live more'n a day er two.

"If'n I didn't see you wasn't from the devil, you woulda ended up the devil's supper, er what was left of ya. Done been nine of 'em ended up thet way!"

Was that why no one who came into the valley left? This madman cut them up with the machette?

"I didn't know anything about this place, three days ago. I heard some tales, but didn't credit them. They say the devil's on the mountain."

"He's here in the valley. Ain't nothin' on the mountain but some kind of ape people. Don't bother me, I don't bother them. Don't much care to go on the mountain. Ain't nothin' there most but mountain."

"Why do you stay here?"

"Uhcause God wants me to keep the devil from goin' out. Uhsides, got a curse on me God's protectin' me from. Got food'n water. Comfterble. Health ain't bad. Better'n most my age. I'm eighty six. Or seven. Fergit exact. See good, hear good. Got it easy!

"I was captin on a ship. Hurricane, I ended here. Nobody liked me, so I came here. God talked tuh me some. I got a agreement. I keep thuh devil in there an' got a easy life. Been here nigh on fifty years. Fifty one. Don't remember exact.

"See, I'm strong. Most what meets the devil is madmen 'n go crazy. I meets him 'n resists what he does, so God knows he can have me an not worry about the devil here. I didn't go looney from seein' him up close, like everbody else. I'm strong! Devil knows he got more trouble then he can handle if'n he gets off his, what I call 'reservation.' Like the Indians, 'n thet, y'know.

"See, I knows these here islands. I was borned on Barbados. Grew up with the devil worship people. Voodoo and magic stuff. They tried to git me dead, but all I got was thet curse. God done stopped that!"

"I see. What happens if they get rid of the devil here?"

"'N he goes somewhere they ain't nobody to control 'im? Anybody thet stupid?

"I guess they is. Sad what people will do."

"Yes. It's really sad to see what the world's become."

"Nother thing! I ain't got to look et thet!"

"Maybe you're the lucky one! I really don't much care for the idea of going back to that. I could stay on this island, I think. It would be okay if you can keep the devil from getting out."

"Done it fer fifty years. Fifty one. Don't remem ber exact. Fifty more, you got to get somebody else. I'll be past it, by then."

"Probably come to that. Nice talking to you, but I'd better get on back. I don't think I'll ever come this way again, but you never know!"

"Yeah, young feller. Good to have somebody to talk to, now and then. Wind ta yer back!" He went into the cave.

Well, that explained part of the reason no one went back from the valley. That tangle of driftwood or whatever answered the rest of it.

If you considered the other reality people as not being a puzzle.

They weren't a puzzle he needed to solve, more than he had.

Now! How to get rid of the devil here!

Did he really want to?

Max came back to the cabin to find Bernadette and Kitti sitting on the porch, waiting for him.

"Did you find why the bridge was there?" Bernadette asked.

"Yes. I've learned some things. I saw what causes the problems in the valley. I have pictures." He took out the camera to show them the shots of the "Driftwood Devil," as he labeled it. They saw the first several, and shrugged. "What?"

He showed the thing where it was at the end of the bridge. Six shots as it rared up.

"Carey says it can't cross the bridge. He's has an agreement with God to keep the devil inside its territory."

"Carey? I'm afraid there's something in that area that prevents me from sensing anything. That's why I didn't know about the bridge – and, apparently, about people being there!"

"Just Carey. Part of why people don't come back is the devil, part is Carey, who thinks they're people the devil sent to take his soul. He knew I wasn't that, because the devil was chasing me."

He told about his experiences. They were surprised Carey was there, and more because he was there for fifty years.

"Do you think we can get rid of that thing?" Kitti asked.

"I don't know. It's not a priority.

"I've been thinking about this situation. Can you tell me where the limits of danger are? I, rather obviously, went into the area of that thing on my first trip through. I told you my route. You seemed to have said you went to the west of where I went, so managed to avoid the places that thing can go. I sensed danger only when the thing was close.

"Can we get a fairly accurate layout, using your talent?

"I know, from Carey, it doesn't go below three hundred feet elevation, and can't go past the rivers east and west, or more than a thousand feet elevation. I want to know the outer design of that area. The perimeters."

Bernadette looked thoughtful. "Do you have paper ... no! You have a computer! Is is WiFi?"

"Yes. I've still got a lot of battery. About an hour and a half." He went inside, to bring the laptop to her. She went to MapQuest, then to another mapping program. She brought up an arial shot of the island, then zoomed in to the area she wanted. She quickly sketched the area, complete with the mountains and rivers.

"So! Did you expect that?" It showed the area Carey described was a very clear triangle.

"To tell the truth, yes.

"Bernadette, the other reality isn't in that triangle. I'm beginning to believe we have two planal distortion points here."

"That is very hard to believe, but there's the evidence!"

"One is hard to believe. Two borders on impossible."

"I think only one. That thing is in the one. The other is a smaller portal," Kitti said. "I sense something, a portent. Bernadette does, too. It's why we waited yesterday and today. The time has a lot to do with it, I feel."

"Time?" he looked at the legend on the laptop. "It's four forty nine, December nineteen, two thousand twelve. That's Nola, so we're more east. Three forty nine."

"Two days," she replied.

"To what?"

"The end."

"End of what? You don't make sense."

"That's the big question," Bernadette answered. "The Mayan calendar. It's not supposed to be the end of the world, only the end that will mean a radical difference to the future of civilization, or something.

"I feel, more and more, that this island is somehow involved."

They discussed it for some time. They couldn't figure what might have happened.

"Well, I still have the rest of my vacation to try to figure something out. I think it would be a good thing to get rid of that thing, but it might not be possible. I imagine more could come, so long as that triangle remains.

"I doubt we could hope to do anything about that. It's not a priority, because getting rid of that could mean we also get rid of the other reality. Our worry is that it's in a place where havoc would break out if it found a way out of it's limits. What if there are thousands of those thing, that they could go anywhere they wanted, here? That's a very scary possibility. It would put us into those stupid BEM movies, for real!

"It's been there for thousands of years, I suppose. Why change it now?"

"According to what I've learned, it's been there for about three hundred years, but it could have been a lot more. There was no one here before that," Bernadette said.

"Not even the Caribbes?"

"I've wondered why they weren't on this island.

It's relatively close to places they settled. It's certainly got everything a primitive society would need! And then some!"

"Shit! I can't go to the elders or whatever to see if there were legends!"

"There are some almost pure Caribbes on Suchando, just fifteen miles from here, by water," Kitti said. "We can go in my boat. Tomorrow at dawn?"

Bernadette grinned. He laughed, and said, "Why the ... heck not!"

The craggy old man, Rosto, tribal elder and historian, of sorts, replied, "We have not gone there since my grandfather seven times removed ruled that there was a hole in the Earth there that swallowed all the people who had lived there since his grandfather, many times removed."

"A great evil," Bernadette said. "We know of a great evil there."

"Evil? No. Just not natural, in this place. It is not in its place, there. It only is. It is not evil nor good. It only is. It is not evil to eat a fish, to the fish. It only is. That is natural. That hole is not natural in that place."

They discussed the island. Max figured the trouble there started three hundred ten or twelve years ago.

Kitti suddenly cried, "Three hundred nine years! It moved three hundred nine years ago!"

"What moved?" Bernadette demanded.

"It. What? What did I say? It was a flash.

"Max, what talent I have is like that. I will say something, and not remember it. We call it a flash talent."

"She will tell a fact that is under discussion. Answer a question about it," Bernadette explained. "It seems we know a bit more about the triangle. It moves. We can hope it moves again, but that will probably be in hundreds of years."

"Just so it doesn't leave that thing here when it does!" Max said. "Also, just so it doesn't move to a place with a lot of population!"

They spent a couple of hours on the picturesque island, made a few friends among the Indians, then went back to Hell.

Hell Island. Max felt he really should differentiate that point!

The questions were answered as much as they ever would be, probably. Might as well enjoy a Caribbean Christmas! Back to the grind would come soon enough.

<u>*A Meeting of Friends*</u>

Christmas day, which wasn't celebrated on Hell Island, Bernadette, Kitti, and Max decided to visit the other reality. They started to go toward the eastern path, but Bernadette said she sensed no danger, whatever. Max had proven they could go a shorter path with reasonable safety. The difficult part was cut away on his original trek.

"I feel there is no danger. That it is ... gone?" Bernadette said. "There is no warning sense at any of the branches in the path."

They were standing by the bridge. Max called, "Carey! It's Max and friends! Are you home?"

There was no answer. They crossed the bridge, and Max called again. Nothing. At the cave, there was no sign of Carey. The fire pit hadn't been used for several days, it seemed. Nothing seemed disturbed.

Max went to look into the cave. It was fairly comfortable-looking. Carey was, as not expected, very neat. It didn't seem that anyone had been in the cave in several days.

There was a big piece of cardboard with a series of figures composed of the four upright lines and a slash across. Numbers. Days, Max decided, when he saw the dates above a line. The top date was Dec. 28, 1961. Each year, starting on January 1, headed a line.

2012 had 71 5-markers. That was ten days short of January 1, 2013. December 21. There was a small piece of charcoal Carey had used for a marker. He wrote short notes on the bottom right of the cardboard. The last one said God told him to go to the gold place today. There were several that said the same thing, some saying he was to go to the rock, or to the wailing tree.

He looked around. There was a box with several pounds of gold nuggets. There were other things collected.

Max went back out. "It seems Carey's calendar ended the same day as the Mayan calendar."

Kitti and Bernadette looked at each other. Bernadette said to bring her something personal from Carey. She had little talent to read such things, but she would know if he was alright or in danger.

Max brought a cup with a little coffee in the bottom. Bernadette looked confused. "He is alive ... but is not? It is cold. He cannot stay there, but he dares not go back. He is hiding, but is not in danger from the thing he is hiding from. It no longer exists?

"It is not remotely possible for us to influence anything concerning him."

They decide to leave things as they were, and to go on. Maybe the questions would resolve themselves.

The portal was still there. They spent two days with Octon and Juli. Several others came. It was a very pleasant meeting, then Max, Kitti, and Bernadette headed back to the cabin.

All-in-all, it was a great vacation! Max was convinced that a very few people did have a psy talent, but not in the voodoo vein. There had been a planal distortion that had moved. That there was a portal on Hell Island to another reality.

That he and Kitti would spend the rest of their lives together in the heaven that was Hell Island.

Max grinned at Kitti, who was fixing dinner. They had the laptop on the World News Tonight from Puerto Rico. He had installed a solar panel to charge the batteries and to run a few lights and such around the cabin. They were more than comfortable there was why they didn't live in the states, or somehwere else.

"It was a year ago tonight when we met," Kitti said. "We have lived ten lifetimes since."

"Yes. We belong together. Fate, and all that," Max replied. "That tastes half as good as it smells, I declare you a master chef!" He turned back to the news.

"... the storm passed without much damage.

"Here's a little thing that fits Halloween! A true puzzle, complete with a monster!

"A scientific crew exploring in the Andes, not far from the southern Peru border, has come upon what they first thought was a frozen tree trunk, on the order of the banyan, which is composed of several intertwined trunks. Upon examination, it was discovered that the supposed tree was an animal of some sort. There is nothing remotely like it that has ever been classified. DNA samples indicate it might not be a life form from this planet!

"That is one for the books! A frozen alien in the Andes! I find it hard to credit. It's probably a hoax ... but this is verified! Very strange!

"A note; the body of a man who appeared to be in his eighties was found nearby. He was dressed in shorts and a worn tee shirt. In the Andes! Far above the permanent ice line!

"Well, Brenda! That seems to be a good kind of story to release on Halloween!"

"Yes, it is, Lorna! I would think it was a hoax, like you, if it wasn't that this is authenticated.

"In other news, President Obama, of the United States, has released a program designed to...."

Kitti, who was looking at the screen over his shoulder, said, "I think maybe the triange has moved to where it won't cause any problems for another three hundred years!"

"We can hope."

C. D. Moulton's works are available on most major outlets as printed or e-books. CD writes the CD Grimes, PI, mysteries, the Det. Lt. Nick Storie mysteries, the Clint Faraday mysteries, the Flight of the Maita science fiction series, books on orchid culture and many others of many types. Mystery, adventure, intrigue, science fiction, humor, fantasy, paranormal, mild erotica, and factual.